Pete the Cat's

BIG DOODLE & DRAW BOOK

by James Dean

HARPER FESTIVAL
An Imprint of HarperCollinsPublishers

Harperfestival is an imprint of HarperCollins Publishers.

Pete the Cat's Big Doodle & Draw Book
Copyright © 2015 by James Dean
For information address HarperCollins Children's Books, a division of
HarperCollins Publishers, 195 Broadway, New York, NY 10007.
www.harpercollinschildrens.com
ISBN 978-0-06-230442-1
15 16 17 18 19   PC   10 9 8 7 6 5 4 3 2
❖
First Edition

The sun is shining!
Draw some cool sunglasses
on Pete the Cat.

Pete loves the beach.
Help Pete build a sand castle.

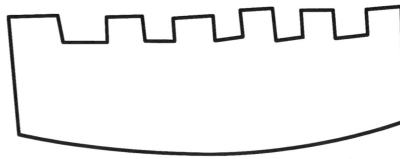

Now help Pete and his friends decorate the sand castle.

Pete doesn't feel cool.
He feels hot wearing too many clothes.
  Put an **X** on the clothes that he needs
to take off.
  Circle the clothes that will keep him cool.

What else will keep Pete cool?

Pete is wearing four white shoes.

Circle the two shoes that are exactly alike.

Answer on page 128

10, 9, 8, 7, 6, 5, 4, 3, 2, 1—blast off!
Pete is heading toward the moon—
but where is it?

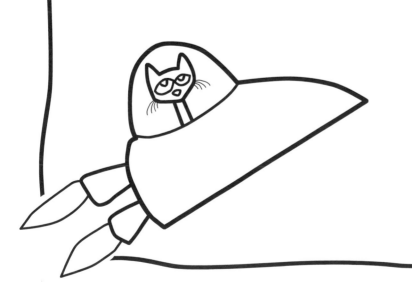

Draw the moon.
Draw other planets
he'll see in space.

Pete rides the bus to school.
The cats on the bus go
meow, meow, meow.
One of Pete's friends goes
woof, woof, woof.
Can you find her?

Pete writes his name.
It starts with the letter P.
Circle the other words that start with P.

Pete

Pig

Cow

Star

Pot

Pencil

Frog

Pete likes to read about dinosaurs.
What do you think THIS dinosaur is doing?
Connect the dots to see.

Pete is rocking out!
Where do you think he is?

Draw a cool background.

Pete's big brother, Bob, checks the weather.
He hopes it will be a great surfing day.
Draw a perfect sunny surfing day in the window.

Bob rides a big wave!
"**Wow!**" says Pete.

Draw some fish swimming in the water.

Pete is daydreaming. Draw what he's dreaming about.

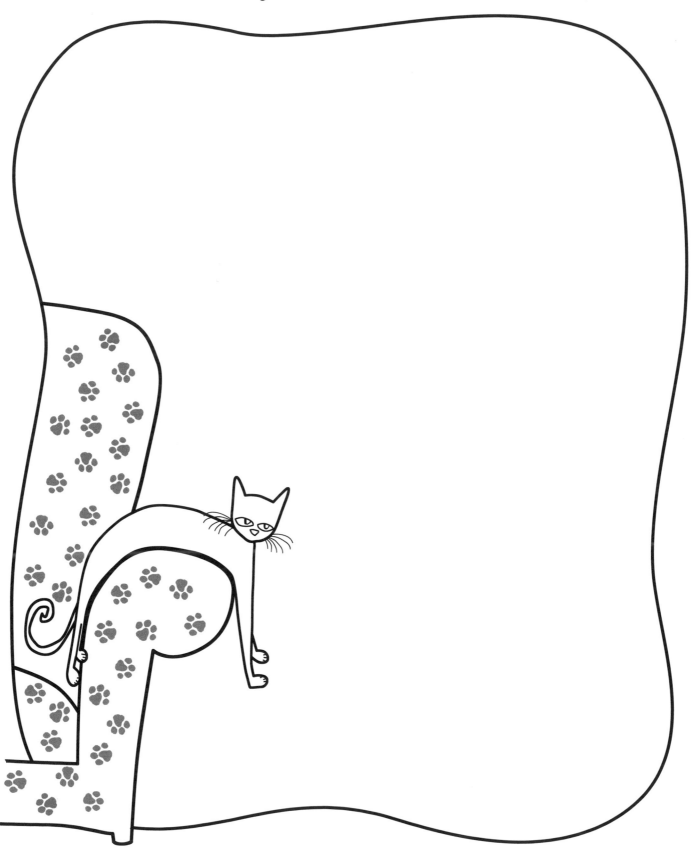

What is Grumpy Toad riding?
Trace the dotted lines.

Pete plays for the Rocks. Decorate their uniforms.

Draw yourself into the game.

Batter up!

Pete whacks the ball over the wall.
Draw a line to show Pete how to
run around the bases for his home run!

Pete's mom is wearing a new
dress. Color it however you like.

Pete's friends ride over to his house—
two on every skateboard.
　　Find the two pictures that are exactly alike.

Answer on page 128

Here is Pete's skateboard, but where is Pete?

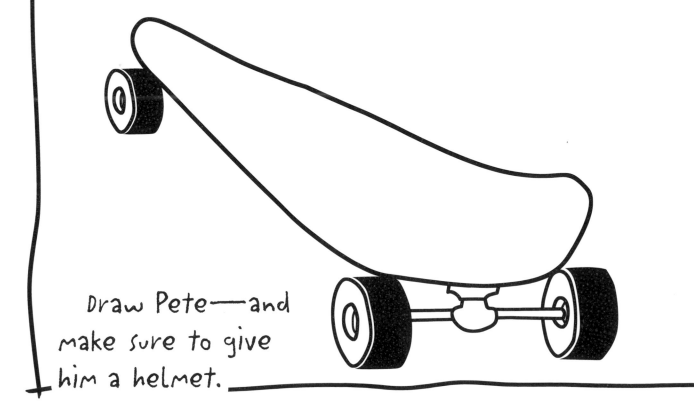

Draw Pete—and make sure to give him a helmet.

Poor Turtle! He is upside down.

Can you draw him right side up?

Pete calls Emma, just to say hello.

Draw a phone
for Emma to answer.

Pete loves his friends. They all like to do different things.

Color Pete's friends.

Pete went so far on his skateboard, he got lost! Help him find his way home.

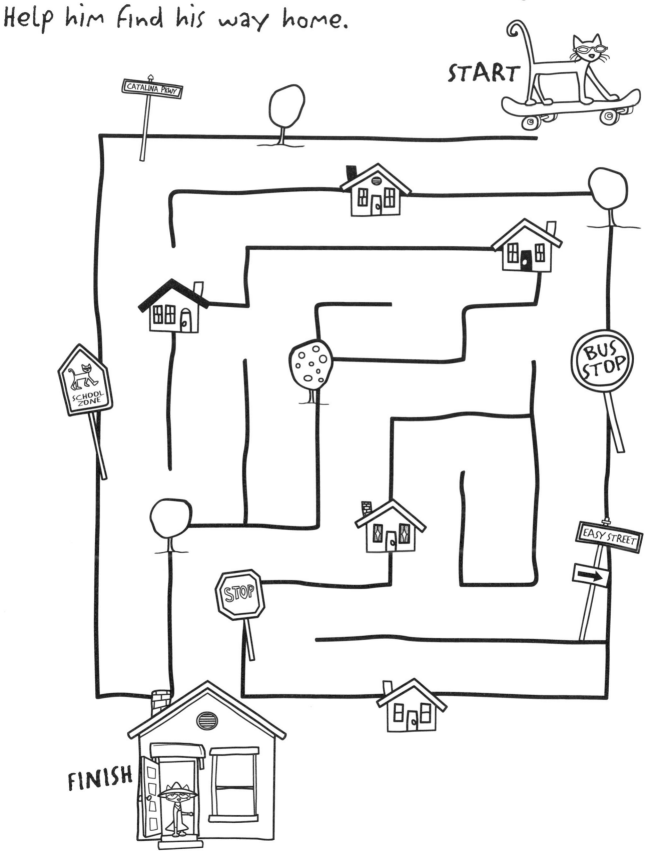

Answer on page 128

Pete has a jar of fireflies!

Color them brightly so they light up the page.

Oh no!
A big wave crashed into Pete's sand castle.
Is Pete sad?

No. Pete's not sad.
He can't wait for you to help him make a new one!
Draw it here.

Pete likes the library.
He wants to read ALL the books—but he doesn't
have enough time today.

Draw the cover of a book that
you think Pete will like most.

Pete is in music class.
The class is practicing for the school concert.
What is Pete playing? Connect the dots to see.

It's time for recess!
What does Pete do first? Connect the dots to see.

Pete loves the playground.
He wants to swing, but there's nothing to hold on to!

Draw what Pete needs.

Pete unpacks his lunchbox.
Almost everything looks delicious.

Which three things don't belong?

Pete draws
a cat.

What does Emma draw?

Pete plants a flag
on the moon!
Decorate the flag.

What would your own flag look like?

The garage is a mess!

Draw a path that will lead Pete to his skateboard.

FINISH

START

Answer on page 128

What a great sunny day!
Pete and Bob are going to the beach with their mom.
Circle the things they will bring.

Which of Pete's friends always gives him good advice?
Connect the dots to find out.

Alligator is hungry.
Draw Alligator's teeth so he can eat his lunch.

Pete likes going to the guitar store.
Look closely and circle the two guitars that are alike.

Answer on page 128

All six of Pete's guitar strings broke! Draw six new strings on Pete's guitar.

Pete is looking through his telescope.
What do you think he sees?

Draw it.

Look! There are six Turtles.
Which two are exactly alike?

Answer on page 128

The cats on the bus shout,

Circle the items that they need for rocking out.

46

Oh no!
The school bus has a flat tire and there isn't a spare.

Can you draw a new tire where it belongs?

Pete likes to paint.
Color his palette.

RED   GREEN   ORANGE   YELLOW   BLUE

Use the colors to make
a picture on his easel.

Crack!

Someone on the Rolls hits a fly ball. Pete tries to catch it, but the birds are in the way. Find and circle the ball. Then count the birds.

There are _____ birds.

Answer on page 128

Two of Pete's friends are playing baseball.

Draw a baseball.

Callie picks a flower for Pete. Color it.

What does Pete give to Callie?
Draw something special.

Pete sees a bunch of eggs.
Where did they come from?
Connect the dots to see.

Pete drew a picture of himself.
Now it's your turn.

Draw what YOU look like.

Pete has cool shoes.

Give Pete a cool hat
and sunglasses, too.

It is a windy day.
Pete is flying a kite.

Decorate the kite however you like.

It's lunchtime! Someone wants to eat Bob and Pete's lunch.

Connect the dots to see who it is.

Draw lunch for the seagulls so they
won't eat Bob and Pete's.

Mrs. Gold, the crossing guard, holds up
a sign so cats can cross the street.

What kind of sign is it?
Color it red.

Mr. Ted is the bus driver.
Today is his birthday.

Make a birthday card that
Pete can give to him.

Pete's mom is hot.
She doesn't want to get sunburned.
Where can she find some shade?
Connect the dots and see.

21
20   1
      2
19   •3

18   •4

17   •5

16   •6

15

      •7
14

      •8
13

12   •9
11   •10

What else is good for shade?

Pete is at the snack truck. What is there to eat?

SNACKS

MENU

Draw some tasty snacks on the menu.

Squirrel is bummed out.
All he could find was one acorn.

Cheer him up by drawing
acorns in the tree, on the ground,
and all around.

Pete opens the refrigerator.
"What's going on in here?" he says.

Circle the things that don't belong.

Pete is super hungry.
He makes a super gigantic
snack.

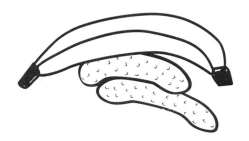

Fill in the spaces
with foods that you like.

Uh-oh! There is a skateboard mix-up.
Match up Pete's friends with their skateboards.

Answer on page 128

Pete and his mom are playing catch at the beach.
Decorate the beach ball with bright colors.

Pete has collected a lot of shells!
Find who is hiding in the pile.
Color him with the rest of the shells.

Poor Grumpy Toad.
He always looks so . . . grumpy!
Give him a smile for a change.

Pete is excited. He is going to visit his grandma.
Draw Pete as he gets ready to get on board.

Bob wears his favorite hat to Pete's baseball game.

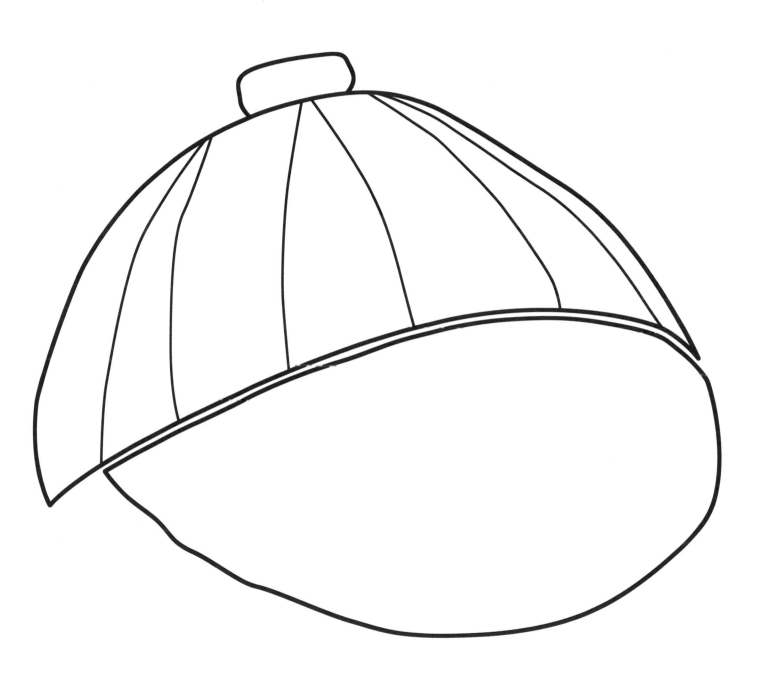

Decorate it with cool colors.

Pete's friend Rob has lots of cars.
"Let's have a race!" says Rob.

Decorate the cars differently so
Pete and Rob can tell which car wins.

Pete's friend Marty loves bananas.
He picks them, eats them, and . . .

Try to guess what
else he does.

Bob and his friends left
their surfboards on the beach.
Only two of them are alike.

Circle them.

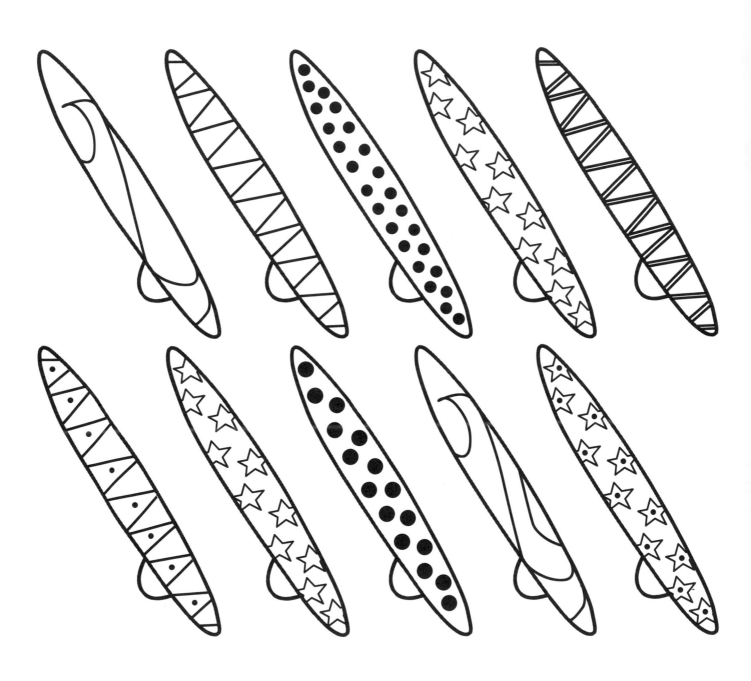

Then color them all in.

Answer on page 128

Oh no!
Pete dropped his buttons in the garden.
Help Pete
find them.

Answer on page 128

Draw Pete and his friends
in the windows of the school bus.

Draw yourself, too!

Hooray! Bob won a surfing contest!
Pete is so proud of his big brother,
he wants to get him a present.

What should
Pete give Bob?

Draw your idea.

Pete is a rock star on a real star!
Fill the sky with stars and musical notes.

Splish! Splash! Pete is taking a bath.
His favorite bath toy is the submarine.
What bath toys do you like? Draw them.

Here are Pete's hats:

Color them in.
Then choose your favorites and draw them on Pete.

Pete has the blue-cat blues.
It's raining and he can't go surfing.

Draw a sunny picture
to cheer him up.

Oh no! Pete missed the bus.
How will he get to school?

Put in the missing numbers on Pete's watch so he won't be late tomorrow.

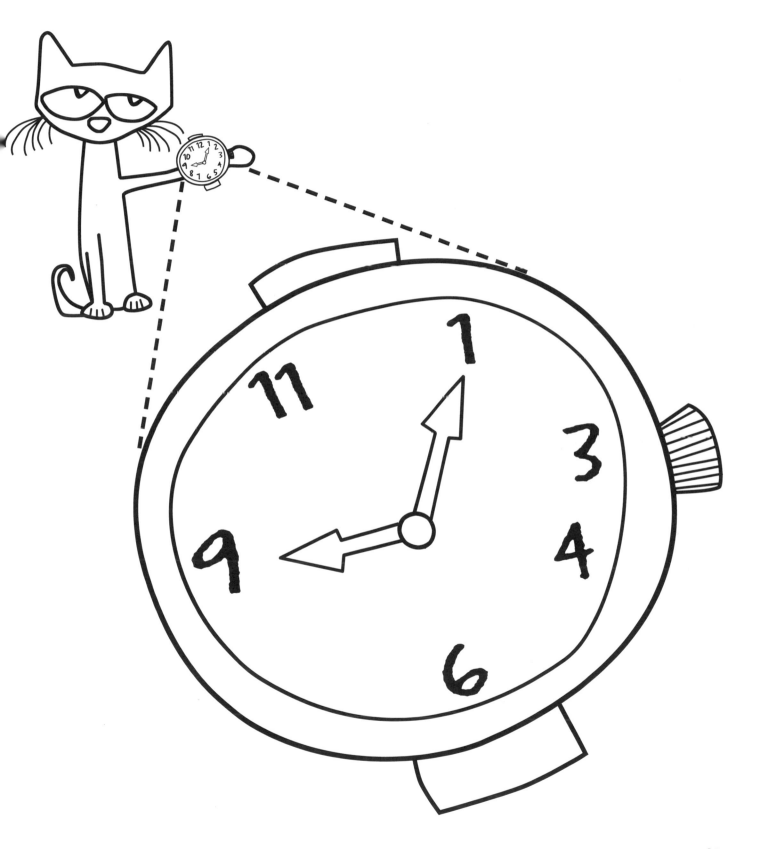

Pete is hot.
Help him find his way
to the ice-cream truck.

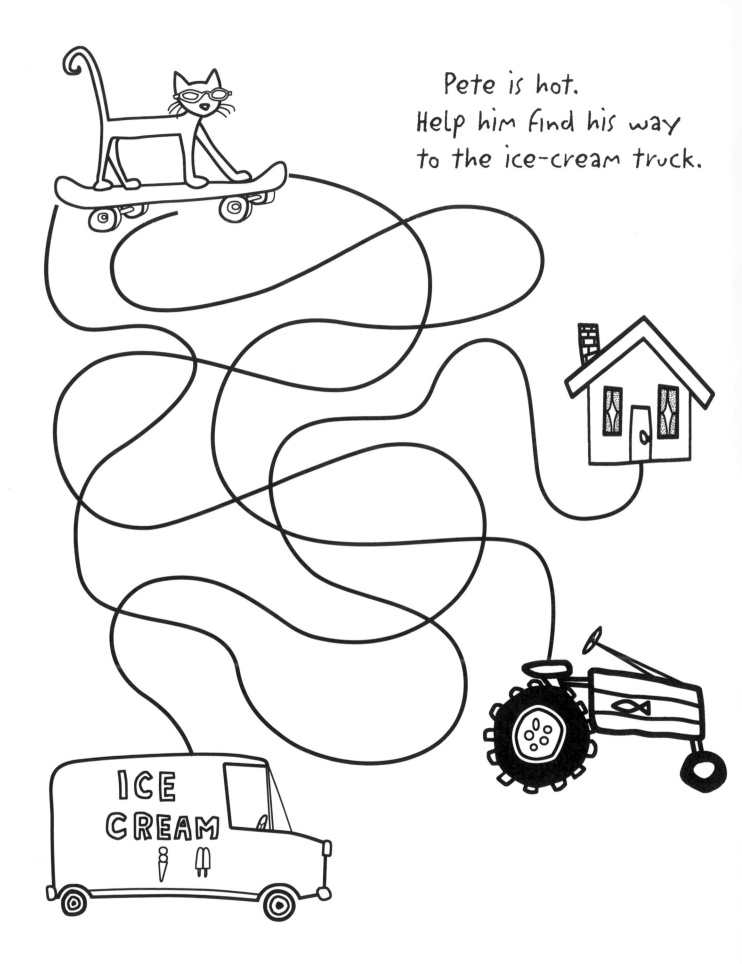

Answer on page 128

Pete can't decide what kind of ice cream to get. Finish the ice-cream cone in Pete's hand so he can enjoy the tasty snack.

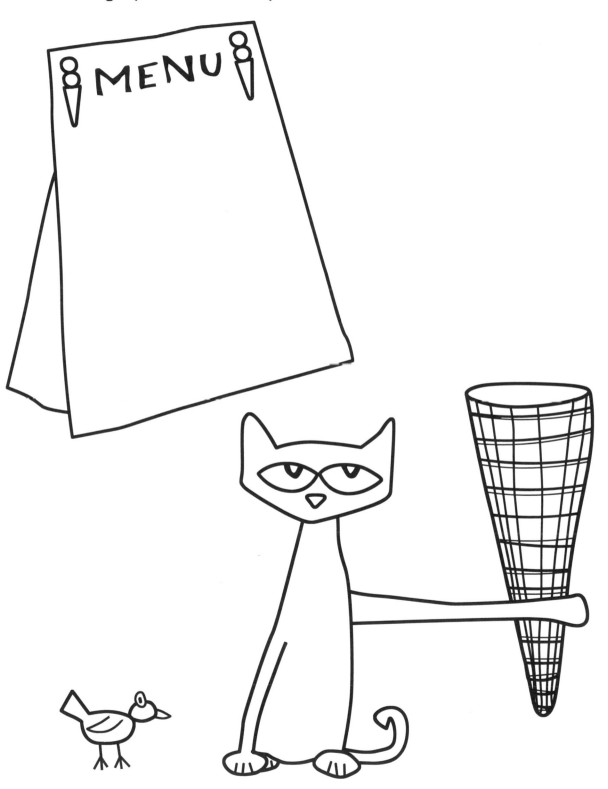

Match up each picture with its opposite.

Answer on page 128

Cool shoes, Pete!
What color are they?

Decorate this surfboard for Pete.

Decorate this surfboard for you.

The waves are too rough for surfing.
Help Pete find his way back to his mom.

Answer on page 128

Pete's band is playing at the beach—
but someone didn't show up.

Draw yourself playing the drums
so you can be in Pete's band.

Pete is wearing
his favorite shirt.
Color it in.

Oh no! Pete's beach ball is rolling away.
Draw a line to help Pete
get his beach ball back.

START

FINISH

Answer on page 128

Pete gave his dirty shoes a bath.
What color is the water now?

Pete and his friends were riding through town when their wheels fell off!

Draw wheels on their skateboards and motorcycle so they can ride again.

Pete's teacher draws the letter S on the chalkboard. "Snake starts with S," she says.

Turn the S into a snake by giving it eyes and coloring it.

Pete is at the store.
He has to get some school supplies.
Circle the things you think
Pete needs.

Bob is at the surf shop.
He wants to buy some cool shorts, but all
the shorts look the same.

Decorate
the surf shorts
with fun colors
and designs.

Pete slides into home.
The catcher tries to tag him out.

What does the catcher have to tag Pete with?

Circle the picture with the correct item.

Pete and Squirrel are playing hide-and-seek.
"Ready or not, here I come!" calls Pete.

Do you know where Squirrel is hiding?
Find and circle him.

Answer on page 128

Pete's team, the Rocks, is getting ready for a team photo—but something is wrong.

Who doesn't belong in the picture?

Bob is surfing. Pete wants to surf, too.
Help Pete find his way through the waves to his
big brother so they can ride the waves together.

Answer on page 128

Pete is on his surfboard, paddling toward the waves.
Draw other things you might see in the water.

Pete wants to drive the bus.
He just needs a driver's license.

Draw a picture of Pete on his license.

The wipers on the bus go
swish, swish, swish—
while Pete drives the bus!

Color the picture of Pete
and all the passengers on the bus.

Pete loves summer because he can surf, skateboard, and drink ice-cold lemonade.

If it were winter, what things might Pete like? Circle them.

Pete is at the playground.
He is looking for his friend Turtle.
Can you find Turtle?

Answer on page 128

Emma is proud to be the only dog in the school.

Draw a picture of her.

Pete goes over a bump with his skateboard.
He starts to fall off.
Draw Pete something soft to land on.

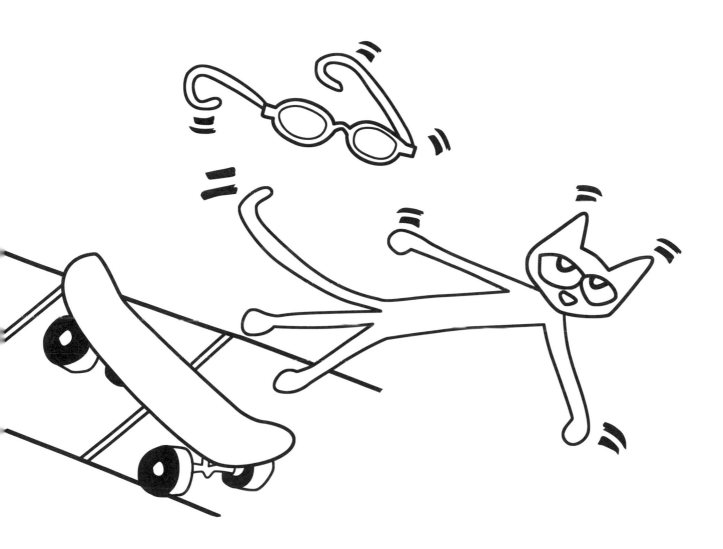

Pete and Bob want to surf,
but the waves are too small.

Draw a big wave for them to ride.

Pete is surfing! So is Bob!

Draw the bright sun shining down on both of them.

Pete is thirsty.
He's squeezing lemons.
What kind of drink is he making?

Draw and color it
in the glass.

Pete and Bob are at the beach.
Draw some boats on the ocean.

Pete's clean white shoes are drying on the clothesline.

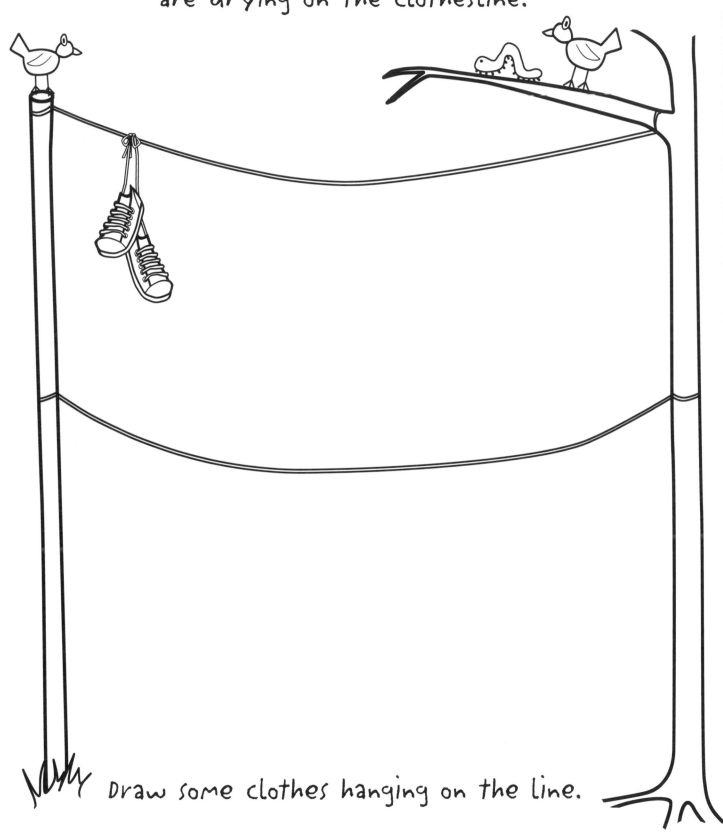

Draw some clothes hanging on the line.

Something smells good.
Pete's mom is making dinner.
Draw the food she's making in the pots.

Pete and Marty are playing follow the Leader.
Draw the monkey bars for them to grab.

Pete's mom baked cookies
for Pete's class.

Draw and decorate them.

It's been a long day.
Pete is getting ready
for bed.
    Design his pajamas.
Draw the things he needs.

Pete's mom reads him a bedtime story.
Draw the cover of the book.

Pete wishes on a star.
What do you think he wishes for?
Draw it.

Draw what you would wish for, too.

Pete can't fall asleep.
He has too much to think about!
   Fill Pete's room with all of his favorite things.

Shh. Pete is sleeping.

Draw what you think he's dreaming about.

Share a snack with Pete.
Draw your favorite food.

Where is Pete?
Draw your own fun scene.

Answers to Puzzles:

page 8

page 21

page 26

page 38

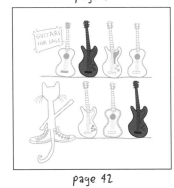
page 42

page 45

page 50

There are __31__ birds.

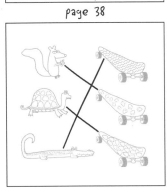
page 68

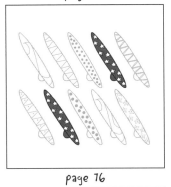
page 76

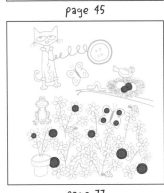
page 77

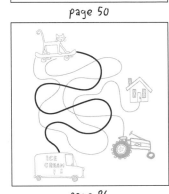
page 86

page 88

page 92

page 95

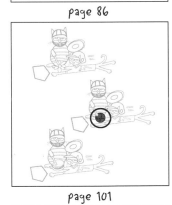
page 101

page 102

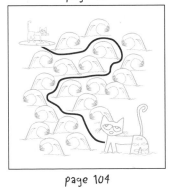
page 103

page 104

page 109